Spike in Space

By Malaika Rose Stanley
Illustrated by Sarah Horne

Tamarind

SPIKE IN SPACE
A TAMARIND BOOK 978 1 848 53096 6

Published in Great Britain by Tamarind Books,
an imprint of Random House Children's Publishers UK
A Random House Group Company

This edition published 2012

1 3 5 7 9 10 8 6 4 2

The Random House Group Limited supports the Forest Stewardship Council
(FSC®), the leading international forest certification organization. Our books
carrying the FSC label are printed on FSC®-certified paper. FSC is the only forest
certification scheme endorsed by the leading environmental organizations,
including Greenpeace. Our paper procurement policy can be found at
www.randomhouse.co.uk/environment

MIX
Paper from
responsible sources
FSC® C016897

Set in 14pt Century Schoolbook

Tamarind Books are published by Random House Children's Publishers UK,
61–63 Uxbridge Road, London, W5 5SA

www.**randomhousechildrens**.co.uk
www.**totallyrandombooks**.co.uk
www.**tamarindbooks**.co.uk

Addresses for companies within The Random House Group Limited
can be found at: www.randomhouse.co.uk/offices.htm
THE RANDOM HOUSE GROUP Limited Reg. No. 954009

A CIP catalogue record for this book is available from the British Library.

Printed and bound by CPI Group (UK) Ltd, Croydon, CR0 4YY

FOR AZIZI AND JOEL

NEWS FLASH!

We interrupt this programme to bring you breaking news and live pictures of a huge alien spacecraft hovering over the town.

Following reports in the press, which questioned whether infant Ali Enson was a 'bonny baby' or an 'alien invader', Thomas J Hoppermann, Director of the UFO Notification Centre, has been bombarded with calls from concerned local residents.

The professor states that his examination of photos and poo prove that the baby is an alien and that his older brother, Spike, made this amazing discovery. However, the boys' parents remain unavailable for comment, leading to speculation that they too are aliens and are responsible for the invasion.

The armed forces have been scrambled and the emergency services are on red alert. The government is urging members of the public not to panic and to stay indoors.

We now return to our scheduled broadcast. Please keep calm and carry on . . .

Contents

Chapter One: The Big Freeze

Chapter Two: Big Brother

Chapter Three: Planet Aledela

Chapter Four: Starting School

Chapter Five: Friend or Foe

Chapter Six: Playing Games

Chapter Seven: Big Bullies

Chapter Eight: On the Run

Chapter Nine: Big Poo

Chapter Ten: Rescue

Chapter Eleven: Home

Chapter 1

The Big Freeze

Spike jumped.

He had never thrown himself off a rooftop onto a waiting spaceship before and he slipped on a loose tile and stumbled. Instead of landing upright inside the pressure chamber, he shot through the air headfirst. He grabbed the lower edge of the door frame with his fingertips, but his legs dangled dangerously. It reminded him of being on the monkey bars in the park – and how hard it was to get across them.

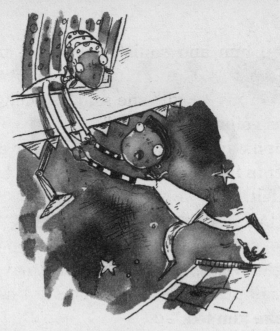

"Oh no!" cried Mum, reaching down to him. "Give me your hand!"

No way, thought Spike. His heart pounded and his arms trembled, but he wasn't letting go. He gripped the platform tighter, heaved himself up and scrambled into the safety of the airlock.

The door clanged shut behind him with a bang louder than his best bass drum boom. Mum threw her arms round him and squished his face into her chest.

"Oh my word!" she said. "I thought I was going to lose you."

Spike heard the mixture of fear and relief in her voice. He knew exactly how she felt.

"Let's go," said Mum, grabbing his hand, even though he was much too big for that sort of thing. "We only have a few minutes left before blast off. I need to take you to Dad."

With her free hand, she jabbed at the buttons on a wall-mounted keypad. The symbols were a weird mixture of hieroglyphics and wingdings. A circular door swished open and they stepped through it into a long, dark corridor.

Spike hesitated. He looked at the silver-grey corrugated metal walls and the trail of faintly-glowing blue lights set in the floor.

3

"It's OK," said Mum, squeezing his hand. "Come on, love."

Spike took a deep breath and followed her. He had only just discovered that his whole family were aliens! And now he was on his way to their home planet. The kids at school would be green with envy, although they might find it hard to believe that his mum was the Pilot and Senior Flight Engineer of an inter-galactic spaceship!

He was having a bit of trouble with that himself. Mum was a daredevil who liked skateboarding and hang-gliding, but she didn't look much like an astronaut. She was still wearing her tatty tracksuit and headscarf. Spike wondered if she would change in time for the launch – maybe into a puffy pressure suit with a huge helmet or a skintight bio-suit, like the ones he'd seen on the telly.

Mum veered off to the left and led him into a room with a shiny, stainless-steel table and a huge freezer. It looked a bit like the kitchen behind the serving hatch in the school canteen. Spike's baby brother, Ali, was nowhere in sight, but Dad had a stethoscope draped round his neck and he was holding a huge thermometer.

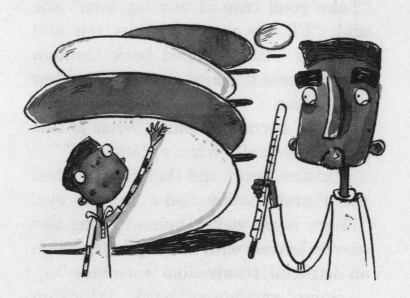

"Hello, big son," he said. "Welcome to the cryo-chamber!"

"Right," said Mum. "I'll leave you both to it. I have to prepare for take-off now and I still need to change Ali."

Spike shuddered. Not another stinky nappy. Yuck!

Mum kissed the top of his head and gave Dad a quick peck on the cheek. "Take good care of our *big* son," she said. "I'll see you in minus ten and counting." She stepped back through the door and it sealed closed behind her with a hiss.

Spike turned to Dad. "What is this place?" he said. "What's going on?"

"Listen, son," said Dad. He crouched down and looked Spike in the eye. "There is no way a human being can survive travelling at warp-speed through an artificial, traversable wormhole."

Spike swallowed hard. What on

earth did Dad mean? Had he changed his mind and suddenly decided to leave him behind?

"The journey to Aledela takes ten Earth years," explained Dad. "No Earthling could cope with the atmospheric and gravitational changes." He took a deep breath. "We don't have a choice. We have to freeze you. We have to put you in a cryo-pod and keep you on ice."

"What?" cried Spike with a stab of panic. "You want to freeze me? Like a mini-pizza or fish fingers or a lolly on a stick?"

"Don't worry," laughed Dad. "On Aledela, we developed cryogenic technology light-years ago. It's perfectly safe. It's just like falling asleep."

Spike wasn't convinced, but beneath his feet he felt the spaceship's engines begin to rumble and hum. It was

too late for second thoughts.

"So which cryo-pod is mine?" he asked cautiously.

"Take your pick!" said Dad.

Spike examined the shiny, different-coloured, metal capsules. They looked like giant M & M's – or Skittles or Smarties. He tapped his knuckles against a flame-blue one and Dad winked at him.

Spike grinned back – but he was totally shocked by what happened next. Dad dunked him in a bath so cold it took his breath away! It was his final memory of his life on Planet Earth.

Chapter 2

Big Brother

Ten Earth years later, Dad unsealed the cryo-pod.

"Big son!" he cried. "My brave space explorer!"

Spike struggled to focus his eyes and squinted up at him. He immediately felt a giggle bubbling up from his belly. Dad's face had a few more wrinkles and his head had quite a lot less hair. He looked older and – well, there was no other word for it – greener!

"How are you feeling?" said Dad. "Are you all right?"

Spike's head felt as if it was full of candyfloss and he couldn't get his brain into gear. He moved his lips, but no words came out of his mouth. And when he tried to sit up, his spine felt like a strand of soggy spaghetti – in a tin of tomato sauce!

"Take it easy," warned Dad. "You've probably got a spot of amnesia and hypothermia. You'll be woozy for quite a while. I've only just taken you out of the turbo-reviver."

"T . . . t . . . turbo?" stammered Spike.

"It's like a giant microwave that heats you up really quickly," said Dad. He peered at the display panel which showed Spike's heartbeat, blood pressure and temperature. "If you thaw out too slowly, you can end up melting into a big puddle."

Spike tried not to panic. He knew he wasn't dissolving. His body felt too bruised and sore. His fingers and toes were tingling. But the heart machine beeped furiously as Dad flicked a switch and the cryo-pod slowly tilted until Spike was standing almost upright.

"OK, big son. Let's get you out of there," said Dad. "Legs?"

"I think so," said Spike. "T . . . two, as far as I remember."

"No," laughed Dad. "I mean, are they working? Or do I need to fetch an omni-wheeler?"

"No way!" said Spike. He had no idea what an omni-wheeler was, but he didn't want to risk any more alien technology just yet. "I think I would prefer to walk."

"Come on, then," said Dad. He handed Spike a warm, dry flame-blue bio-suit and a shiny, silver foil blanket. "Let's get you up to the flight deck."

Spike leaned on Dad's arm and took his first few rickety steps out of the cryo-chamber.

"I wanted to defrost you in time for the descent because that's the most thrilling part of every space voyage," said Dad. "You missed the flight through the wormhole, but that's basically just a long tunnel and there isn't much to see."

They shuffled along the metal corridor and Spike gradually felt the warmth and strength coming back to his arms and legs.

"So how do you make a wormhole anyway?" he asked. "And how does the spaceship travel through it?"

"We have an on-board particle accelerator," explained Dad. "We use it to smash atoms and open the wormhole.

Then we use the power of the explosion to propel the spacecraft."

Spike nodded, but he didn't say anything. He wasn't sure he would ever get the hang of advanced alien astrophysics!

They approached a set of zigzag-shaped, reinforced double doors. Dad tapped a hiero-dings code into the keypad and they parted to reveal the flight deck.

Spike gasped. It was a vast, brightly-lit bubble, and right in the middle Mum was sitting in front of a huge bank of displays and controls. She was wearing a stretchy, all-in-one lilac spacesuit – and a new headscarf – but the curls poking out from under it were speckled with silver. Like Dad, she looked older – and greener. As soon as she saw him, she sprang up and raced across the flight deck.

"Welcome back, love!" she cried, giving him a big bear hug and spinning him round till he was dizzy and his legs wobbled again. She guided him to the seat next to hers in the centre of the cabin. "Thanks, honey," she added, glancing back at Dad and blowing him a kiss. "I knew you'd get him here all in one piece!"

Spike gazed at the view through the wide-angle cockpit window. For the first time, he could see that he really was travelling through the cosmos.

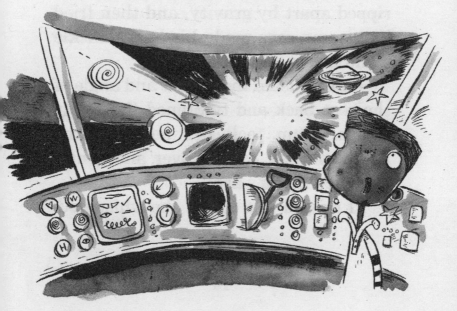

Against a background of deep, dark blue, there were twinkling clusters, glowing spirals and shining swirls of billions of beautiful stars. There were huge clouds of gas and dust, glowing with red and neon-pink light or reflecting the dazzling blue of the nearest stars. There were soft blobs of dark, velvety black, but not like the ones he had learned about on Earth when he had researched UFOs.

Spike shuddered. The very idea of being sucked into a black hole and ripped apart by gravity, and then fried by gamma rays made his knees buckle – and he sat down.

Dad adjusted the height and angle of the seat back and tightened the safety straps. Mum took her hand off the flight controls, leaned over and gently squeezed Spike's arm.

"I missed you, love," she whispered.

"I'm so glad we are all together again."

"Except for Ali," said Spike. "Where is my baby brother, by the way?"

"Hi, bro!" called out a voice from the other side of the cockpit. "I'm no baby – not any more!"

The voice belonged to a boy dressed in a bio-suit similar to his own. He swivelled round in his seat and waved, and then went back to flicking switches and twirling dials on the control panel.

Spike gaped. The boy did look a bit like Ali. He had the same twinkle in his eyes and the same crooked smile. His brown skin had more of a greenish sheen than Spike remembered, but his whole family seemed to be getting greener the closer they got to Aledela. Or maybe the green increased with age. The last time Spike had seen his little brother he had only been six months old! He had been rolling around in a carry-cot, bellowing at the top of his lungs and demanding a bottle or a clean nappy. But the boy he was looking at now was just a year or two younger than himself.

"Don't look so surprised," said the boy. "Remember, you have spent ten years in a cryo-pod. You haven't changed a bit!"

He laughed – the same gurgling chuckle he'd had from the moment he was born. Spike's mouth dropped open as he realized that this really was his *baby* brother, Ali.

"I've been growing – and learning stuff – for ages," said Ali. "Size-wise, I've nearly caught you up. Brain-wise, I bet I've—"

"Stand by for re-entry and landing!" yelled Mum, before Ali could say anything else.

Ali quickly turned back to the control panel and Dad rushed to take the seat next to him. Spike stared, speechless, at his adopted alien family. He only managed to tear his eyes away from them when he caught his first, distant glimpse of their planet through the cockpit window. Aledela IV. His new home.

Chapter 3

Planet Aledela

Spike gazed down and saw that one side of the planet was in total darkness.

"That's the western hemisphere!" said Ali, showing off his advanced knowledge of the planet's geography.

The other side, which even Spike now knew was the eastern hemisphere, was bathed in a soft, yellow glow. It lit up the weird gold and purple shapes of the land, and the different shades of turquoise of the lakes and canals.

"That's Ledel light from the planet's star!" said Ali, showing off his advanced knowledge of the planet's solar system.

Aledela was stunning, thought Spike, but there was no time to admire it. Their descent had begun. Instead of gently floating through space, they had entered the planet's atmosphere and were suddenly plummeting towards it.

Spike dug his fingernails into the armrests as he was slammed backwards against his seat and all the air whooshed out of his lungs. The enormous g-forces pummelled his body and rattled his bones. It felt like being on the most hair-raising, stomach-churning roller coaster ride in the whole universe.

"Deploy descent thrusters!" ordered Mum, bellowing over the deafening engine noise and the sound of Spike's half-excited, half-terrified screams. "Jettison heat shield!"

Dad's mouth and green-flushed cheeks flapped wildly, and Ali's nose was squashed flat and his green-tipped ears were pressed against his head as the ship gathered more speed.

They both frantically flicked switches, pressed buttons and turned dials.

"Extend landing gear!" yelled Mum, as her green bloodshot eyes bulged. "Deploy radar!"

Spike's heart pounded with the same rhythm and force as the pulsed firings of the descent thrusters. But the spaceship made a touchdown as soft as a falling feather and he puffed out a huge sigh of relief.

It was suddenly deathly quiet too and Spike wondered if he had actually died – or whether it was just because his ears needed popping! He retched – and reached for the safety belts strapping him to his seat. Vomit comet! Puke nuke! Spurt alert!

"We haven't docked yet," said Mum, with a soft sigh of her own. "Just hang on until we reach the spaceport."

Spike nodded and swallowed very hard as he waited for the all clear. He was probably looking a bit green himself by now. His head was spinning. He felt wobbly and weak – and he still couldn't speak.

"Bro!" exclaimed Ali, bouncing up from his seat and bounding across the flight deck to high-five him. "Awesome, wasn't it?"

Absolutely, thought Spike. As long as hurtling through space, being squashed to a pulp and rattled into a jibber-jabbering wreck counts as awesome!

Spike stumbled out of the airlock and into the spaceport, which buzzed with activity and excitement. He scrunched up his eyes against the dazzling Ledel light and stared out at the cool, one-person space-jets, sleek passenger starships and enormous cargo transporters lined up on the launch and landing pads.

"Come on!" cried Ali, racing ahead. "Let's get moving."

Somehow, Spike made it through the space terminal without falling flat on his face, even though he kept spinning round and gawping at everyone. Aledelians shared many of their physical features with Earthlings, but it was hard not to stare at the snazzy shaved or shaped designs of their hair – and at the colour of their skin which ranged from emerald and teal to lime and jade.

He followed his family to a line of small, driverless vehicles that seemed to hover in the air.

"Transport pods," said Ali. He swiped his hand across a smartcard reader just inside the sliding door and pointed to the web of skin between his first finger and thumb. "ID, GPS and RFID."

Spike shook his head, not understanding. There were so many things he didn't know. So many things he had to learn. He was glad his baby brother had a head start and that he was here to help him.

"Everyone has a microchip transponder," explained Ali. "Dad implanted mine on the spaceship. It's an all-in-one radio frequency identity card, galactic positioning system, interstellar passport and pre-payment card."

"Does it hurt?" asked Spike nervously.

"Not much," said Ali. He winked and Spike wasn't sure whether or not he was joking.

"No worse than when I had my ears

pierced on Planet Earth," said Mum, noticing his doubts and trying to make him feel better.

The card reader plotted their route and the transport pod whizzed them along an invisible skyway. From the interactive GPS map on the display screen, Spike could see that they were headed towards the centre of town.

He gazed down at the city, stretched out in all directions beneath him. Most of the buildings looked like a giant version of the 3-D set he had used to learn geometric shapes at school – cones, pyramids and cylinders. Some were upside down and others floated above the ground. They were built from huge glass blocks and sand bricks, decorated with multi-coloured spirals and swirls. There were solar panels and wind catchers on the roofs, which were linked by invisible skyways. On the ground, there were purple parks and golden gardens, criss-crossed by a network of turquoise canals.

Far off in the distance, at the edge of the city, there was a wide, dark-blue strip of farmland. Beyond that, there was nothing but desert and then the jagged mountain range which marked the border between the light and dark sides of the planet.

"Bro!" yelled Ali. "See that big octahedron-shaped building over there with the roof garden on top? That's the academy. That's where we will go to school."

Spike whirled round to look. Everything was happening so fast, he could hardly believe his eyes or catch his breath. This was the adventure of his life! His heart was bursting with excitement, but his head was spinning in confusion.

How on Earth – or Aledela – did Ali know what an octahedron was? How did he already know about the academy? While Spike had been packed inside a tin can and refrigerated, Ali must have spent the whole time studying extra-terrestrial geometry and geography – as well as learning how to fly a spaceship!

"I'll be in a higher class than you,"

said Ali, guessing what he was thinking. "On Aledela, kids are graded according to what they know and what they can do instead of their age."

Spike sighed. Then he gasped at the sight of the flock of huge birds suddenly flying alongside them. Their bodies were covered with curly tufts of multi-coloured fluff and they had long, twisty, spiral-shaped beaks. Instead of wings and tail feathers, they seemed to have rotors or blades on top of their tiny heads and sticking out of their enormous bottoms.

"Heliraptors!" cried Ali, just before the transport pod

slid to a halt outside a pyramid-shaped building.

As they left the pod, Spike stared at the huge glass prism on the roof that formed rainbows in the sky as the Ledel light shone through it. It was actually the lift, which transported them down through the centre of the building to their apartment.

Inside, the high-tech design was all based on circles. In the family area, there was a kitchen with food and drink dispensers and a round table, semi-circular sofas and a curved, wall-sized media screen. The hydro room had a wrap-around steam shower – and an alien digestive system waste disposal pod! Spike knew that was what it was just from the smell. It reminded him of the huge amounts of stinky, gut-wrenching green poo Ali had produced when he was a baby. Yuck!

Spike was a bit disappointed to see that there were only two sleep areas, which meant he would have to share with Ali. But at least they had separate sleep pods with what looked like sliding screens to block out the chatter of know-it-all younger brothers.

"I'm zonked," said Spike, climbing into one of the pods. He plugged in his headphones, turned up the volume on his XP7 player and snuggled under the silver-foil cover. "It's been a big day."

"Deca-beat!" bellowed Ali, turning up his own volume to correct him. "It's been a big *deca-beat*."

Chapter 4

Starting School

The next deca-beat, Spike was woken by the sound of Mum banging on his sleep pod screen.

"Spike!" she called. "You have to get up. Your father and I have been called to an urgent meeting at the space institute. You and Ali will have to go to the academy."

Spike turned over and groaned.

"Sorry, love," said Mum. "I know you probably need a lie-in and we were planning to show you around, but it's out of our control. Come on, it's breakfast time. We don't want to be late."

Spike buried his head under his pillow. Unbelievable! Mum and Dad were making him go to school on his very first day – or deca-beat – on a brand-new planet! To be honest, after what Ali had said, Spike didn't care if he never set eyes on the academy ever again. What could be worse than starting a new school and ending up in a lower year group than your little brother? It wasn't fair.

"Spike!" shouted Mum. "Did you hear what I said?"

Spike sat up and slid open the screen. "I heard you," he yawned, shielding his eyes from the sudden glare of Ledel light.

He crawled out of the pod and followed Mum to the kitchen. Dad and

Ali were already washed and dressed. They were sitting at the table, tucking into bowls of what looked like frogspawn topped with mutant fruit. Mum said it was sago porridge, but she didn't explain why all the fruit was dark blue, purple – or even black. Spike decided it must be something to do with alien photosynthesis and the way the fruit trees used the Ledel light to grow.

"What do you fancy, big son?" said Dad. "Tangelo? Pomelo?"

"Try a tamarillo," said Mum. She helped herself to an egg-shaped shiny blue fruit, cut it in two and gave Spike half. "They are really tasty – tangy and sweet."

Spike took a bite. It tasted like a mix of rotten eggs and boiled broccoli and he spat it straight back out!

"Ugh!" he cried. "Yuck! That is totally gross!"

Ali laughed so hard he nearly fell off his chair. Even Mum and Dad glanced at each other and giggled.

"Sorry, love," said Mum for the second time that deca-beat. "I should have warned you not to eat the skin."

Spike scowled. She didn't look sorry.

She couldn't keep the silly grin off her face, like the rest of his family.

"Doesn't matter!" he snapped. He slid his bowl of sago across the table and stomped off towards the hydro room. "I'm not really hungry anyway."

Spike stood in the shower, steaming. He could do without his family making fun of him! He was already worried enough about going to school and whether he would fit in. Would the other kids like him? Would he make any friends? What if he got lost? Or abducted by an alien?

After a while, he vaguely heard the sound of Dad shouting over the noise of hissing steam and gushing water. Spike turned off the shower and stepped into the whoosh of warm, dry air in the body dryer. It was only a little bit quieter.

"Come on, big son!" yelled Dad through the door. "Mum and I are due at the institute. After all our time away, we have to report back on our Special Project for the Investigation of Kids on Earth."

S.P.I.K.E. That would be me then, thought Spike gloomily. Why couldn't they have given him a normal name – like Joel or Azizi – instead of labelling him like a research project? He pulled on his bio-suit and opened the door.

"At last," said Dad. "We are all going to be late."

Spike shrugged. He didn't really care. He barely noticed when Dad pressed a small piece of plastic into his hand.

"It's a radio frequency identity card," said Dad. "You will have to use it until we can fit your hand with a micro-transponder. You'll need it to register as a student at the academy, to buy lunch, to programme a transport pod when you want to come home and to unlock the apartment door. Don't lose it!"

"OK," said Spike, slipping it into his pocket.

"Listen, big son," said Dad. "Your mother and I know this is all a bit rushed and it's not fair on you, but the space investigators are desperate to hear what we have learned from Earthlings." He put his arm round Spike's shoulders and gave him a squeeze. "Try to enjoy yourself, all right? Don't worry about Ali. He's all talk. Don't forget, it's his first deca-beat at a new school too. He's just as nervous as you."

A little later, Spike stepped out of a transport pod and trailed after his little brother, who practically skipped into the academy. A few kids were milling around the top floor entrance hall and almost all of them fell silent and stopped what they were doing to stare at him.

Spike felt a rush of Earthling blood to his head. For the first time, he realized he was the alien! He was the one who was different. It was him who would have to get used to living on a new planet.

"Hi," said Ali, smiling and looking around hopefully. "Can someone tell us where we have to go to register?"

An emerald-skinned girl approached them. She offered her hand in a gesture of welcome, but instead of shaking it, Ali gently stroked his palm sideways across the back of her hand.

Spike was impressed, even though he didn't want to be. With his green-tinged skin, Ali blended in already. He certainly hadn't wasted any time on that spaceship. On top of everything else, he must have been learning how to impress the girls! He introduced himself and he looked as if he knew exactly what he was doing when he almost forgot to mention Spike. If he was nervous, he was making a really good job of hiding it.

"Hi," said the emerald girl. She stroked Ali's hand and then greeted Spike in the same way. "I'm Nyra." She turned and signalled to a boy who looked so much like her, Spike was sure they must be twins. "And this is my brother, Aryn."

"The reception area is over there," said Aryn, looking them up and down and then nodding his head to the left. He gave them a friendly grin, but didn't bother stroking hands.

Spike and Ali followed his line of vision. The entrance opened onto a grand hall with a high ceiling and lots of doors leading off it. There were sofas and chairs balancing on springs, clustered round the registration desk, and an art display of *Dangerous Alien Monsters* on the wall, which cheered Spike up and made him laugh.

Aledelians really did have a lot to learn about Earth. They had drawn or painted pictures of cuddly kittens and newborn lambs!

Ali swiped his hand over the card reader on the reception desk and Spike did the same with his RFID tag.

The information was automatically scanned into the academy computer system. The administrator tapped an icon on his touch screen and one of the doors swished open. A woman glided across the reception hall to meet them. She had pointed hair and fingernails, which looked as if they had been dipped in Earthling blood. Her mouth was painted to match. She looked like a scary vampire, but Spike's eyes were drawn to her bright-red convertible wheelchair.

He stared at the gleaming aluminium frame, shiny chrome alloy wheels, titanium footplates and red leather, body-shaped supports. It reminded him of the prototype cyber-trax sports car he had once seen back on Earth. If this was an omni-wheeler, thought Spike, he wished he had accepted Dad's offer to ride on one. It obviously had a powerful engine because the woman zoomed towards them in no time at all.

"Welcome!" she said. Her voice was friendly and she gave them a big smile, which made her seem a lot less scary. "I'm Principal Zellez. We have been expecting you."

"Nice wheels," said Spike, before he could stop himself.

"Thank you," said Principal Zellez. She did a tight 360° spin, followed by a wheelie, balancing effortlessly on the single trailing back wheel.

Then she pushed a button on the armrest and the machine transformed itself into a wheeled standing frame. She slapped the joystick arm away and stroked their hands before turning to the administrator's computer screen and scrolling through the information.

"Spike and Ali Enson," she read aloud. Her moss-coloured brow crinkled. "I see you have both assimilated the lingua galactica from familial interaction."

"Pardon," said Spike, not understanding a single word.

Principal Zellez grinned at him. "Oops, sorry," she said. "What I mean is that you have picked up the Aledelian language just from talking to your mum and dad."

Spike shrugged. He had grown up speaking two languages, but he had never really thought about it before.

It didn't seem like a big deal. It was the same for a lot of the kids he knew at his school on Planet Earth. They used English at school, but at home they spoke Punjabi, Yoruba, Albanian, Somali, Aledelian or whatever.

"I understand you have lots of techno experience too," said Principal Zellez, looking at Ali and frowning even harder. "But you need to catch up on cosmostory and a few other basics, so for starters I think we will put you both together in the tyro grade."

Spike sighed with relief, but he heard Ali mutter something about the *baby class* under his breath in frustration.

"Do you already know any other students who you would like to show you around the academy?" said Principal Zellez.

"Nyra," said Spike, quick as a flash.

"Perfect," said the principal. She

tapped a hiero-dings icon on the computer screen and glanced back at Ali. "I'll team you up with Aryn then, shall I?"

"Thank you," said Ali in a quiet new-kid-at-school voice.

Spike secretly grinned. He felt better already. But for Ali, things were not going exactly according to plan.

Chapter 5

Friend or Foe

"You know what?" said Nyra. "I'll get study credits for showing you around even though I am missing astrometry."

"Is that a good thing or a bad thing?" asked Spike.

"Very good," said Nyra. She flashed a smile, which made her purple-flecked eyes sparkle. "I prefer astrobotics."

Spike smiled back, but he didn't say anything. He was worried. So far, he hadn't even heard of any of the subjects taught at the academy. On Earth, his favourite subject had been music. He was an awesome drummer! He even had his hot-rod drumsticks tucked inside his bag, but he wasn't sure now was the best time to mention it. He decided to be patient and wait for the perfect moment. Then he would offer to play her one of his top-ten favourite drum solos.

Nyra started the tour on the ground floor so that Spike could have a proper look at the academy from the outside. Ali was right – it *was* a giant octahedron. It had a triangle-shaped floor and roof, and six triangular walls built from the same glass blocks and multi-coloured sand-brick cubes as most of the other buildings. Inside, Ledel light shone down through the ten-storey-high glass roof, and circular escalators twisted and turned up to each floor.

Spike soon realized he was more interested in Nyra than the guided tour. He tried to focus as she pointed out the different laboratories, studios and workshops, but he couldn't keep his eyes off her emerald skin and short twists of blue-black hair. He tried to concentrate as she gave him the lowdown on all the teachers, but mainly he just listened to her chirpy sing-song voice.

Nyra was smart. She remembered to show him where to find the boys' waste disposal pods – although he reckoned he could have followed his nose and found them all by himself! She even timed the end of the tour so that they were first in the queue for lunch!

Spike was starving. He hadn't eaten breakfast – and it was ten years since his last proper meal! He dug the RFID tag out of his pocket and scanned it to pay for a triple portion of purple potato chunks with blue tomatillo dip, and an extra-large carton of pomelo juice. He staggered under the weight of his tray as he followed Nyra up the final spiral escalator and out onto the roof garden. They sat opposite each other on curvy metal  benches in the shade of a gigantic purple pot plant and were gradually joined by some of her classmates.

"My best friends," said Nyra as she introduced them. There were four girls and two boys, including another set of twins. They were full of questions.

"Where are you from?" said Aynya.

"Earth," said Spike.

"Greetings, Earthling," joked Kerek. "We come in peace."

Spike joined in with the laughter. He wasn't used to being the centre of attention, but this was fun. On Earth, boys sometimes thought he was a bit of a loner – and he didn't usually talk to girls at all! He had always felt more of an outsider than he felt now, as an actual alien.

"We've been learning about Earth," said Orinel. "We found out that Earth-lings communicate by tapping their fingers on little black or silver boxes."

"Oh, yes," said her brother, Leniro. He laughed. "And they travel around on the ground in big, multi-coloured rolling cubes!"

"And they trade for things with

pieces of coloured paper and metal discs," said Amelema, shaking her head in disbelief.

Mobile phones, cars and money, thought Spike after a moment.

"How long are you here for?" said Isokosi. "Are you staying here for good?"

Before Spike had a chance to answer, a much bigger, older boy stood in front of them, blocking out the Ledel light and casting a long, dark shadow.

"No, he's not!" snarled the boy. "He doesn't belong here!"

"Go away, Rodor," said Nyra. "Go away – and grow up."

"Stay away from him!" warned Rodor. His eyes narrowed. "And don't stick up for him – not if you know what is good for you. We already have enough alien space invaders! We don't need any more!"

Spike was stunned. Enough aliens?

More aliens? He had thought he was the only one!

Rodor's raised voice attracted attention and a few other kids drifted over, including Nyra's brother, Aryn. Spike stared around at them. For the first time, he realized that some of them weren't green! One girl was pale blue.

Another was the same shade of brown as himself. A couple of the boys were a reddish pink colour. Spike felt a shiver of recognition. They were aliens, just like him – although he was pretty sure they weren't Earthlings. One had lizard skin and the blue girl had pointed ears and a swishy tail!

Rodor grunted and Spike glanced back at him. Mum reckoned most Aledelians were gentle and peace-loving, but there was nothing gentle about Rodor. He was out for alien blood and looking for a fight! The atmosphere on the roof was tense.

"What's the matter, alien boy?" challenged Rodor. "Can't you speak for yourself?"

Spike had plenty to say, but most of it was rude and he wasn't sure it would be a good idea. He looked around for his brother – for backup or guidance –

but Ali was all on his own on the other side of the garden. He was staying well away from any trouble and keeping to himself, but he was watching carefully. At this distance, Spike wasn't sure if the look in Ali's eyes was worry or bravery.

"What's your problem, Rodor?" said Leniro. "Why don't you just leave him alone?"

"What's it to you?" growled Rodor.

"He's a friend," said Aryn. "Back off!"

"A friend?" said Rodor. "So soon? How sweet!" He laughed nastily. "And here was me thinking he was just some sort of strange creature from outer space!"

"He's an Earthling!" cried Nyra, leaping up from the bench to stand shoulder to shoulder with her brother. "Do you have a problem with that?"

"Problem?" Rodor's grey-green face

folded into a sneer. "The way I see it, you lot are the ones with the problem, but don't worry. I promise to sort it out. Trust me, this isn't over."

It wasn't a promise, thought Spike gloomily as he watched Rodor swagger away. It was definitely a threat.

Chapter 6

Playing Games

"How was school?" asked Dad later.

"Brilliant," said Spike. "It was great."

"Boring," said Ali. "It was grim."

Dad did a double take.

"I met this girl called Nyra," said Spike. He felt a warm friendly glow, quickly followed by an icy shudder as he remembered Rodor. "And then I met a boy who was really—"

"We met loads of kids!" said Ali, cutting him off. He glared at Spike and silently mouthed the words, "Shut up."

Spike frowned. Who died and made Ali master of the universe? It was true Spike could deal with any trouble on his own without whingeing to Mum and Dad, but that didn't give Ali the right to boss him about! He was still his *little* brother.

"They put us *both* in the tyro grade," said Ali grumpily.

"Ah," said Dad. "That explains everything."

"So how did you and Mum get on in your meeting?" said Spike, swiftly changing the subject.

"Also brilliant," said Dad. "As far as the space institute is concerned, you are already a bit of a star."

"Him?" said Ali. "A star? How come?"

"The investigators are very excited about what we can learn from Earthlings," said Dad.

"What could anyone learn from Spike?" said Ali. "He can't even fly a spaceship!"

"You are a quick learner, kiddo," said Dad. "You have great technical skills and you'll make a terrific pilot some day, but Spike is just more . . . well, he has great personal qualities."

"Like what?" said Ali.

"He's loyal and kind," said Dad. "He's brave and adventurous – and tougher than he thinks. It sounds like he coped really well with being different to everyone else on his very first day at a new school. Not everyone could do that."

Spike beamed. He could practically see Dad's chest bursting with pride. His own chest felt the same, but he didn't want to make a big deal of it. He didn't want to be a show-off, like Ali.

"Maybe what Aledelians and Earthlings need is a mixture of both," he said modestly. "A bit of technology and a fantastic personality."

"Spot on, big son," said Dad. "Well said."

The next deca-beat, Spike attended his first proper class. It was astrography, which he had found out was not quite as scary as it sounded. Basically, it was just Aledelian geography. Ali had managed to convince Principal Zellez he was some sort of astrographical genius and she had agreed to bump him up to a higher grade. Without anyone to show him the ropes or keep him company, Spike felt nervous. He swiped his RFID tag over the computerized register next to the classroom door and then just stood there with what he hoped was a friendly grin plastered across his face. Once again, everyone stopped to stare at him, but he was getting used to it.

There was an empty seat next to a pea-green boy at the back of the lab. Spike walked over and sat next to him.

"Hi," he said, offering his hand to the boy. "I'm Spike."

"I know who you are," said the boy. He edged his chair away. "I know what you are too."

Spike got the message. He wasn't green, but so what? He knew there was no point trying to explain where he came from. The grumpy lump sitting next to him was twice his size and much older, yet here he was still in a tyro grade astrography class. He had probably never even heard of Planet Earth!

Spike grabbed his bag, ready to move places, but he was too late.

"Be seated," ordered a robot teacher

as it clattered into the lab. "I am Aza 5* and class has begun."

Spike groaned and slumped back into his seat, but he soon forgot about the grumpy lump. Aza 5* turned on the media screen and Spike plugged his virtual-reality headset into the desk console and immediately found himself floating around in cyberspace.

Compared to Earth, Aledela was very small, and compared to the sun, Ledel was even smaller – and really cool! The planet was in what Earthlings called the *Goldilocks zone*, where conditions for life were 'just right'. It made a full orbit of the Ledel star every ten deca-beats, but it did not rotate. That was why there were no seasons or days and nights – and why one side of the planet had water, warmth and light, but the other side was dry, cold and dark.

"Pip," said Aza 5* as the lesson ended. "Please stay behind. I would like to speak with you."

Spike sighed. For a moment, he thought the robot teacher had got his name wrong. Then he realized the grumpy lump was called Pip and he only just managed to stop himself laughing out loud.

During the lunch break, Spike met up with his friends on the roof.

"How's it going?" asked Nyra.

"Awesome," said Spike.

He had decided follow Ali's orders after all and not to blab to anyone about his problems with Rodor – or with Pip. After all, he was meant to be brave and adventurous. He was tough! It was better to concentrate on the good stuff.

"Do you want to play oopupoo?" said Aryn.

Spike shrugged. Here was something else he'd never heard of!

"Go on," said Nyra. "It's good fun."

Aryn threw the oopupoo towards him. It was squidgy and soft. It took on a streamlined teardrop shape in the air, but moulded itself to the shape of his hand when he caught it.

The game didn't have many rules and it didn't take Spike long to pick them up. At first it was just him, Aryn and Kerek against Leniro, Navan and Iggi. But when they'd finished eating, the girls joined in too. Then the lizard-skinned boy he'd seen earlier, whose name was Xorg, and a few other *space invader* aliens. In the end, there were about fourteen or fifteen players on each team.

Points were scored when the oopupoo crossed the centre line. It was harder than it looked, and Spike was bounced around till he was dizzy. He knew he was letting Aryn and Xorg and the rest of his team-mates down, but no one seemed to care. Nyra was right. It was fun. It was just a shame his team was on the wrong side of a seventeen–nine thrashing.

Chapter 7

Big Bullies

A few deca-beats later, Spike left the musi-cosmology studio at home time and went to meet Ali. Spike was in the advanced music class because of his outstanding talent. Ali had been put in the tyro grade with the beginners – which had also helped to put him in his place! The brothers didn't hang around together much at the academy, but to keep Mum and Dad happy, they had agreed to meet up every day for the pod journey home.

Spike searched the entrance and reception halls. Ali was nowhere to be seen. As usual, he was being a total pain in the you-know-what – and Spike was going to tell him so. But, of course, he had to find him first.

Halfway up the twisty escalator to the roof, Spike heard Rodor shouting followed by the sound of jeers and laughter. And then he heard a blood-curdling shriek of pain from Ali!

Spike raced up the last few steps. He gaped at Rodor and the circle of bully boys surrounding his little brother! Ali was trapped in the middle – cowering and fighting back tears – but making no attempt to escape. For a moment, Spike was frozen with shock. Then red-hot rage exploded inside him and he burst into action.

"Get away from my brother!" he

screamed as he shot across the garden.

He hurled himself at the nearest boy, who happened to be Pip.

A searing pain, like a bolt of electricity, shot through his body. Ali was being held inside some sort of force field! Spike had taken Pip by surprise and broken through, but the energy field shattered like shards of glass and Ali was violently flung to the ground.

The bullies backed away – all except Rodor. He looked Spike up and down and then turned to his mates.

"Come on, guys," he said scornfully. "Our work here is done."

The boys laughed and it was only the sight of Ali curled up in a heap at his feet that stopped Spike trying to take on the whole lot of them. He watched them leave. Then he dropped to his knees and reached out towards his brother.

"Don't touch me!" said Ali, shrugging him off. "I don't need you to rescue me."

Spike looked at Ali's face. His left eye was bruised and puffy, there was a graze on his cheek and a trickle of green blood oozed from his split lip.

"You are totally messed up!" said Spike.

"I can look after myself," said Ali, standing up and wincing with pain.

"Are you sure?" said Spike. "It doesn't look like it."

Ali's eye was already swelling shut, but he still managed to glare at Spike before he clutched at his ribs and hobbled away.

They didn't talk the whole way home.

"In the name of Ledel light!" cried Mum when she saw all the blood and bruises. "What happened? Who did this to you?"

"No one," muttered Ali. "It's nothing."

"Nothing?" echoed Mum, turning to Spike for an answer.

"I'll fetch the first-aid box," said Spike miserably as he trudged off to the hydro room. He knew Ali would be even

71

more mad at him if he told Mum what had happened.

Mum cleaned up Ali's face, dabbing away the blood and daubing the wounds with a foul-smelling ointment. Ali gritted his teeth and didn't say a word except for the occasional "ow" or "ouch" and Mum didn't ask any more questions.

It made Spike feel nervous. He couldn't concentrate on his astrometry homework or music practice and by dinner time, he had totally lost his appetite.

"So how was school?" said Dad, breaking the awkward, gloomy silence round the table.

"Fine," said Spike.

"What about you, kiddo?" said Dad, still staring in horror at Ali's ointment- and blood-streaked face. "How was your deca-beat?"

"Fine," mumbled Ali.

Dad looked at them both for a long time. "Your mother and I have been thinking we should pop into the academy and have a word with Principal Zellez," he said at last.

Spike held his breath and waited to see how Ali would react, but he didn't say or do anything. There was just

another long silence, interrupted only
by the sound of Dad sadly slurping soup.

Later, as he climbed into his sleep pod,
Spike wondered if Mum and Dad
thought he had bashed Ali! He would
never do that! But maybe that was why
they hadn't demanded an explanation.
Maybe they thought they could sort
things out between themselves.

Spike sighed. Seeing Ali being bullied
was worse than being picked on himself!

"Ali," he whispered. "Are you still
awake?" Ali didn't answer, but Spike
pressed on anyway. "What was all that
about?" he said.

"Nothing," said Ali at last. "Forget
it. I can take care of myself."

"I know," said Spike. He hesitated.
"So what happened?"

"I was sticking up for you," muttered
Ali.

At first, Spike thought he hadn't heard right. Then he felt as if he had been whacked round the head with a sand brick!

"Standing up for me?" he said quietly.

"They were calling you horrible names and saying terrible things about you," said Ali.

"Oh, great!" said Spike. "And all you had to do to make them stop was let them trap you in a force field and make fun of you?"

"I knew you wouldn't understand," said Ali.

"I do understand," said Spike. "I'm just surprised you were defending me."

"I just want us to fit in," said Ali miserably. "I just want us both to belong."

Spike sighed. He didn't know what to say. He knew exactly how Ali felt. He lay there, listening to the sound of his brother's breathing until he was sure he had fallen asleep. Then he slipped out of his sleep pod and crept through the apartment. He needed to talk to Mum and Dad.

They were still up. He could hear them talking, but something about their low, secretive voices made him hesitate and listen in. He peeked through the crack in the door to the living area. They were snuggled up together on the sofa.

"Maybe it was a mistake to bring Spike here," whispered Mum.

"We couldn't leave him behind!" said Dad.

"Oh, honey," said Mum. "Of course not, but perhaps it would have been easier for three Aledelians to fit in on Planet Earth than for one Earthling to fit here on Planet Aledela."

"You're right," said Dad. "I don't think we had much choice, but maybe we made the wrong decision for Spike and for Ali. It will be hard to make him go back."

Spike gasped and clapped his hand over his mouth. His heart did a triple back-flip! He stared at his parents in disbelief. He waited for them to call out and tell him off for eavesdropping, then collapse with laughter and admit that they were just sharing a joke.

No such luck! They weren't even smiling. Spike tiptoed away. He had heard enough!

It wasn't just Rodor and Pip who didn't want him around. It wasn't just Ali being bullied that he had to worry about. With Mum and Dad's help, he was sure he could sort that out. But that was never going to happen. His own parents didn't want him here. They wanted to send him back!

Chapter 8

On the Run

Spike yanked on his bio-suit, grabbed his RFID card and fled.

Outside the apartment, he blinked and shielded his eyes. Of course, he knew that Ledel light shone constantly, but he was still surprised by how bright it was even when he would normally be sleeping. Instead of heading for a transport pod, Spike took the steps. By the time he reached the ground floor, he was running full-

pelt – desperate to get away.

He raced along the walkways and sprinted over the canal bridges. He had no idea where he was heading, but he fixed his eye on the jagged ridge of mountains and kept going until he reached the outskirts of the city. His burning lungs and pounding heart finally forced him to slow down, but his scrambled thoughts and feelings refused to let him stop. He couldn't stay if he was putting his brother in danger! And he wouldn't stay where he wasn't wanted!

Spike put one foot in front of the other and kept plodding through fruit orchards, vegetable plots and sago palm fields, which stretched right and left, as far as he could see. It looked a bit like the farmland and countryside on Earth, but in completely the wrong colours. He shook his head. It was better not to think about the planet he had left behind.

After a while, Spike noticed a drop in the temperature. The farms gradually gave way to dry, dusty desert. The mountains loomed up, silhouetted against the sky. It was darker too, but without a rising or setting sun it was impossible to judge how long he had been gone or what distance he had covered. All he knew was that he was hungry and thirsty – and that he needed to rest. Spike peered through the gloom across the rippled sand. In the distance, there was a single, spindly tree and he trudged towards it. A gust of wind blew down off the mountains. It whipped up the sand and stung his face. He screwed his eyes closed and stumbled down onto the cool, gritty sand. He leaned against the narrow trunk and tried to decide what to do next.

He could carry on in the same direction and climb up into the mountains or he could turn round and walk back to the city. Spike swallowed hard as he realized he was too exhausted to do either. He didn't even have the strength to stay furious with Rodor and Pip – or with Mum and Dad. If he was still angry with anyone, it was himself.

He should have known better. If

he was going to run away, he should have prepared properly. He should have brought camping equipment and supplies. He should have made a plan. Of course, thought Spike miserably, the best plan would have been to stay at home! Running away from his problems wouldn't solve anything.

Spike shivered in the wind. He buried his face in his hands and tried to pull himself together.

When he looked up again, he noticed for the first time that the ground was scattered with shiny, egg-shaped, blue fruits. He was sitting beneath a wild tamarillo tree – and it was actually sagging under the weight of the ripening fruit!

Spike crawled around on the ground and stuffed himself stupid. He broke open the skins and sucked out the sweet, tangy fruit. When his belly was full, he

started to fill his pockets for later. His fingers closed around his RFID card. He took it out and looked at it. It was no good to him now. He tossed it aside and continued filling his pockets. He had enough for two or three meals – more if he was careful.

Spike burped – and he felt the ground shake beneath him. OK, it was deep and loud, but it wasn't powerful enough to set off what felt like a landslide or earthquake – or Aledela-quake! He sprang to his feet – and almost fell over again in shock. In the distance, he caught sight of an animal, moving fast and charging towards him! The creature's eyes glittered in the gloom – and all three of them were firmly fixed on Spike.

He hoped it was something cute and furry that just happened to enjoy running. But he knew it wasn't. As it pounded the ground and hurtled closer, he could see that it was huge and hairy, with vicious-looking spikes on its head and tail. One head butt or tail swipe from this beast and that would be the end of him!

Spike glanced around, thinking fast and desperately looking for somewhere to hide – or for something to use as a weapon. Then he came to his senses. He was in the middle of a desert! There was nothing except a few boulders and the spindly tamarillo tree. He probably wasn't strong enough to lift a boulder, never mind use it to bash a monster. He glanced up at the tree. This was definitely a *monkey bar* moment!

Spike bent his knees, sprang upwards and grabbed hold of the lowest branch. It was easier than he expected. Either he had misjudged the height of the branch or he was bouncier and taller than he remembered. Maybe he'd grown!

He tightened his fists round the branch and swung his legs up behind him – just as the monster smashed headfirst into the trunk, shaking another huge pile of ripe fruit from the tree. For a moment, the animal was stunned by the impact and it lumbered blindly away.

But Spike watched in horror as it turned around, snorted and pawed the ground, and got ready to charge again. He realized that if he didn't make his getaway right now, the next thing shaken out of the tree would be him. He leapt down and ran for his life!

He didn't know whether the beast was chasing him. He was too terrified to turn round and look and the only sounds he could hear were the crunch of loose stones beneath his own feet and the blood throbbing inside his head. He ran until he tripped over a small boulder and ended up sprawled on the hard, rocky ground.

He glanced behind him, in a panic. Thankfully the monster was nowhere in sight. Spike felt his grazed elbows and knees through the holes in his bio-suit as he lay on the ground, panting and trying to catch his breath.

He felt a huge a wave of exhaustion roll over him. He closed his eyes and fell into a deep sleep.

Chapter 9

Big Poo

When Spike woke up, he felt the comforting warmth of a fire. He heard the flames crackle and pop. For a moment, he wondered whether being chased by a three-eyed, spiky-horned monster had just been a terrible nightmare.

He opened his eyes and looked around. He was still in the middle of the desert, but instead of stones and sand, he was lying on a pile of sago palm leaves. The cuts on his knees and elbows had been smeared with some sort of paste.

A few metres away, an old man was bending over the fire and poking it with a stick. He moved slowly and Spike reckoned he could almost hear his bones creaking. He seemed to sense that Spike was watching him and he slowly straightened up and turned round.

Spike immediately saw the effects of living without Ledel light. The man's skin was wrinkled and faded – more khaki than vibrant green – but his eyes were huge and they lit up and sparkled like emeralds when he smiled.

"How are you feeling?"

"OK, thanks," said Spike, easing himself up into a sitting position. "Thirsty."

The old man put down his stick and brought him some water. Spike gulped it down and immediately felt better. He was glad the man had found him and he felt safe from the monster, but he was curious. Who was he – and what was he doing out here in the middle of nowhere?

"I am Deved," said the man, answering Spike's unasked question. "I am a wanderer."

"A wanderer?" said Spike, cheering

up and feeling more at home. "My name's Spike. I'm a wanderer too. Maybe I can stay here with you."

"And maybe triceragons can dance in the sky!" laughed Deved, setting a bowl of food in front of him.

No chance, thought Spike. Not if that's what the head-butting tail-swiper had been. There was no way a monster like that could dance – or fly.

"You are welcome to share my food and my fire, but you cannot stay," said Deved. "You don't belong here. You have to go back to the Ledel light side."

"I don't belong there either," said Spike. "I ran away. My family are probably glad to see the back of me."

"That micro-transponder in your hand is transmitting your location," said Deved. "I expect your family are searching for you as we speak."

"No transponder," said Spike, holding

up his hands in a gesture of surrender. "No RFID tag either. I chucked it away."

Deved laughed again. "I don't think that will stop them."

The porridge or soup – it was hard to tell exactly what it was – tasted bitter and slimy and it was scalding hot. It burned Spike's tongue but he blew on it and ate it gratefully.

"Can you throw a bit more fuel on the fire?" asked Deved a little later.

Spike was glad to help, but he hesitated. What he'd thought was a pile of logs was actually a heap of dry, brown lumps that looked – and smelled – like poo!

"There are no trees in the mountains and only a single tamarillo tree here in the desert," said Deved.

Spike returned Deved's smile. He knew he was lucky to have found the tree at all.

"I use triceragon dung as fuel for my fires and lanterns," explained Deved. "I use their milk to make butter and cheese and I use their wool to make clothes and blankets."

Spike tried to imagine Deved shearing a triceragon like a sheep or goat – or even a llama or alpaca. He would need ropes and pulleys or a ladder. It would be like trying to shave a woolly mammoth!

"Aren't you scared of them?" he asked as he shifted a couple of lumps of dung to a better position to dry in the wind. "One of them charged at me and I thought I was going to be killed."

"Did you stare into its middle eye?" said Deved.

"I stared into all three of them," said Spike. "With no fire, it was darker than it is now. I was trying to work out what it was."

"That was your first mistake," said Deved. "Didn't anyone ever tell you that it is rude to stare?"

Spike suddenly realized he was staring at Deved and he quickly looked away and stared into the flames.

"Did you have food?" said Deved. "Did you offer to share?"

"You must be joking! I thought it was going to eat me!"

"They don't eat us and we don't eat them," said Deved. "That was your second mistake. Triceragons are sociable herbivores. You should always invite them to dinner."

Spike stared at him again. Was he serious?

"Did you run away?" said Deved.

"Too right!" said Spike. "I was terrified."

"Mistake number three," said Deved. "You can't expect a triceragon to let you take away its dung if you hurt its feelings."

Chapter 10

Rescue

Spike lay on his pile of sago palm leaves in the dark. Like the triceragon, he knew all about hurt feelings. He felt as if there was no one in the whole universe who cared if he lived or died.

He rolled over onto his back and stared up at the stars. Somewhere up – or out – there was Planet Earth. He had spent a lot of time wishing he had never left or that he could go back – but why? He didn't have any real friends there.

He had always told everyone, including himself, that he preferred to be on his own.

But now he really was alone, Spike realized he didn't like it at all. He didn't want to be a wanderer, like Deved. He wanted his mum. And his dad. He needed a friend. Maybe even his little brother.

An idea exploded in Spike's head like a sonic boom! If he was honest, Mum and Dad weren't the sort of parents who would adopt an alien kid, drag him halfway across the universe and then forget all about him. The same went for Ali!

Spike made a decision. Running away had been a big mistake. He missed his family. He was going home!

He said thank you and goodbye to Deved and set off across the desert – away from the mountains and towards the Ledel light.

Before long, he spotted the wild tamarillo tree – and sitting beneath it was a whole bunch of kids from the academy, including Ali and Nyra. And Rodor and Pip!

Spike could hardly believe his eyes. He remembered his discarded RFID card. They must have tracked the signal. Spike tramped towards the tree, kicking up sand and stones, but no one heard him coming.

They were all too busy stuffing themselves with fruit. They were too busy shouting and arguing about Spike.

"We are never going to find him," said Orinel. "It's time to give up and go home."

"No way," said her twin brother, Leniro. "He has to be here somewhere. What if he is lying in a ditch injured and starving?"

"It's not like anyone kidnapped

him," said Rodor. "He just upped and left!"

"What choice did he have?" said Aynya.

"Anyway," snapped Isokosi. "He left because of you!"

"Chill out," said Pip. "We've already said we're sorry."

"It's not us you need to apologize to," said Amelema.

"Just stop it!" snapped Ali, leaping to his feet. "If we keep this up, we'll never find my brother!"

Spike kept walking towards them, and at the last moment Ali caught sight of him and their eyes met. Ali did a double take and his eyes opened wide in surprise.

Spike looked back at his little brother. He was only ten metres away, but somehow it felt like ten light-years. There was nothing he could do about it though. Not yet anyway.

At that very moment, over Ali's shoulder, he could see a triceragon! It was charging across the desert straight towards them! Spike's stomach did a triple back-flip. Somehow, with his brother and the other kids in danger, the creature looked even more terrifying than when he had been alone. Its head was low. There was fire in all three of its eyes. It was making a horrible, snorting growling noise.

Ali whirled round to see what Spike was staring at. He panicked.

"Get up!" he screamed at the others. "Run for your lives!"

"No!" yelled Spike as they all scrambled to their feet. "Don't run! Don't run!"

Everyone ignored him. They raced past him and almost knocked him off his feet in their desperation to get away. Rodor and Pip were shrieking and squealing with fear. They didn't look so tough now.

Spike's heart hammered in his chest as the triceragon thundered towards him, closer and closer. He forced himself to walk towards the tamarillo tree. His legs trembled. His palms were sweaty. But this was a matter of life and death. He scooped up as much fruit as he could and held it out towards the triceragon. The ground shuddered and shook beneath him as the enormous beast bounced and skidded to a halt.

Spike stooped down to lay the fruit at the monster's feet. He glanced up, careful not to stare into the creature's middle eye. It was breathing hard. It snorted hot air – and bad breath – straight into Spike's face.

Now was the moment of truth. Would the triceragon charge – or come for tea?

Had Deved been speaking the truth or lying through his teeth?

Spike slowly turned his head to see if Ali and his friends were still there. They had fled to the edge of the desert and they were huddled together behind a sago palm.

As Spike turned back to face the triceragon, he smiled as he realized he had thought about them as friends. And unbelievably the triceragon seemed to smile back at him! It greedily gobbled up the fruit – and pooped! The stench was so disgusting it almost knocked Spike off his feet. He was tempted to hold his nose, but he didn't want to seem rude. He stood perfectly still, squeezed his eyes shut and held his breath instead.

The triceragon stamped the ground and bellowed.

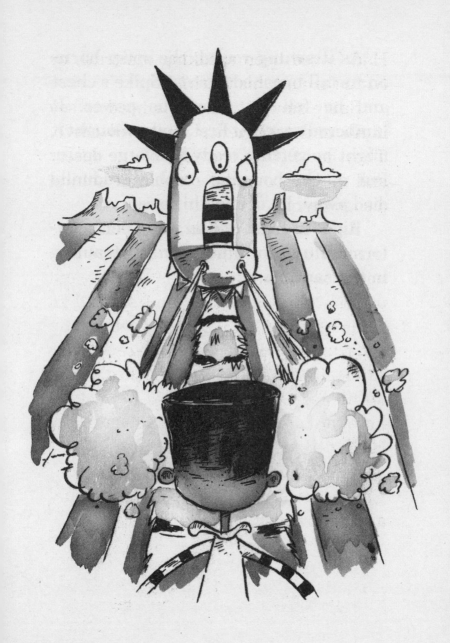

As it swung round, the spiky horns on its tail brushed against Spike's chest and he felt its enormous power. It lumbered away. At first, Spike thought it might be getting ready to charge again. But as the booming rumble gradually died away, he opened his eyes.

Right in front of him was a perfectly-formed lump of dung, gently steaming in the sand.

Chapter 11

Home

Spike raced over to his friends. His eyes swept over the rescue party. Everyone was there – Nyra, Orinel, Leniro, Xorg, Kerek, Isokosi, Aynya and Amelema – and Ali.

Nyra threw her arms round his neck and hugged him – Earth-style!

"That was amazing," she said. "How did you do that?"

Spike froze. Over her shoulder, he had spotted Rodor and Pip again. They

were both still cowering behind the sago palm!

"What on Aledela are they doing here?" he asked, without answering her question.

"We didn't come to cause trouble," mumbled Rodor. "We . . . er, we volunteered to help look for you."

"We wanted to make up for how we treated you and Ali," said Pip.

Spike stared at Rodor and Pip for a long time. He wasn't sure if he believed them – or whether he could trust them.

"They didn't exactly decide all by themselves," said Amelema.

"Right," said Nyra. "Ali stood up to them. He warned them there would be trouble once the two of you stuck together."

Spike looked at his brother. His chest flooded with the same swirling mixture of feelings he remembered from their last night on Planet Earth, when Ali was still a tiny baby. Brotherly love – and huge relief.

"It's t . . . true," stammered Pip. "And, er . . . thanks for saving us from the m . . . monster."

Spike and Ali laughed – and their friends joined in.

"No problem," said Spike. "But you had better make sure you behave yourselves from now on. If I can see off a triceragon, I can definitely deal with you!"

Mum and Dad flung open the apartment door before Ali could scan his micro-transponder. They must have heard the transport pod approaching. Dad's face was so pale it had only the faintest hint of green and Mum's eyes were puffy and swollen.

"Why did you run off?" yelled Dad,

glaring at Spike. "And why didn't you tell us you were going off to look for him?" he shouted at Ali.

"I heard you talking about sending me back, but I don't want to go to Earth without Ali," said Spike.

"And I don't want to stay on Aledela without Spike," said Ali.

"Spike," said Mum, shaking her head. "We were talking about sending Ali back to school, not sending you back to Earth."

"And none of us would stay on Aledela without Spike," said Dad, rolling his eyes. "Although the truth is, it doesn't really matter where we are, kiddo, as long as we stick together."

"And as long as you are both OK!" cried Mum. She pulled them into a hug and then quickly pushed them away again so she could look them up and down. "You *are* OK, aren't you?"

"Well, we were all nearly trampled by a huge, hairy triceragon," said Ali. "But Spike saved us!"

That wasn't quite the whole truth. Spike knew he could never have managed it without Deved's help, but there would be plenty of time to explain that later.

"My poor darlings," said Mum, sweeping them up into her arms again. She kissed the top of Ali's head and tried to do the same to Spike. She stood on tiptoes, but she still couldn't reach and she stared at him in surprise. He really had grown!

"Kiddo! Big son!" said Dad, leading them down the curved hallway towards the family area. "I don't know what we would do if anything happened to either of you."

Spike sighed. As far as Mum and Dad were concerned, there was no difference

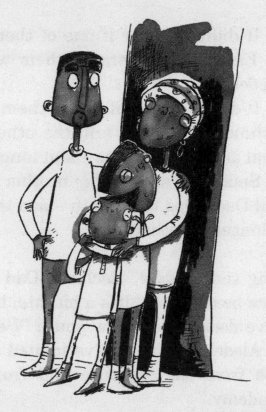

between their sons apart from a few years in age – and a few centimetres in height!

It didn't matter if one of them was adopted and one of them was their bio-child.

It didn't matter if one of them was an Earthling and one of them was an Aledelian.

It didn't matter if one of them was a technical whizz-kid and the other was loyal and adventurous – and tough.

Spike was still the *big* brother. Mum and Dad loved them both – and they all belonged together.

"Big son! Kiddo!" declared Dad a few deca-beats later. "It's a bit late, but we have decided to throw you a 'Welcome to Aledela' party. We've invited everyone from the institute and from the academy."

Everyone? That meant Rodor and Pip and the rest of their gang as well as his own crowd, thought Spike. He really hoped it would be a chance for them all to make friends.

The first guest Spike spotted was

Principal Zellez. She was sitting on one of the semi-circular sofas while a group of kids from his astrography class took turns to ride her wheelchair.

"You should give it a go," said Principal Zellez, raising her glass of pomelo juice in a toast. "It might be your last chance before your mother fits it with a particle accelerator. We're going to try our hand at omni-racing!"

Spike glanced across the room at Dad.

"Don't worry about your father," smiled Principal Zellez. "He just wants some peace and quiet to meditate and find his inner alien."

Ali handed Spike his hot-rod drumsticks. "I know you were only gone for one deca-beat, but I was looking after them for you."

Spike grinned as he realized he wouldn't swap his little brother for all

the stars in the universe. He even tried
to give him a hug, but Ali wriggled away.

"Whoa!" cried Ali. "Save the mushy
stuff for your girlfriend, bro. Go and
play her a drum solo."

Spike sat down at his drumkit, which
Ali had unpacked and set up in the

corner of the family area. His drumming was a bit rusty. He hadn't played a solo since his last night on Earth. He took a deep breath and started with a soft, steady beat on his bass drum. He slowly built up the rhythm with the tom-tom and snare drums and gradually added the cymbals. As his confidence grew, he increased the speed and volume to really show off his skills. His audience clapped and cheered and Spike brought his performance to a close with a flourish – a final crash of cymbals and a big bass drum boom!

"That was brilliant," said Nyra. "Why didn't you tell me you could play the drums?"

Spike laughed before he even managed to crack the joke.

"Well, I didn't want to bang on about it," he said happily.

About the author

Malaika Rose Stanley grew up in Birmingham.
She has worked as a teacher in Zambia, Uganda,
Germany, Switzerland and Britain. She is now
a full-time writer and the Royal Literary Fund
Fellow at the London College of Fashion. She
also runs creativity and writing workshops
for children and adults. Her publications for
Tamarind include *Baby Ruby Bawled, Skin Deep*
and *Spike and Ali Enson.*

Malaika enjoys travel, singing, reading, ballet
and football. She lives in North London near her
grown-up sons.

About the illustrator

Sarah was born one snowy November day
in sub-zero Derbyshire, UK. She graduated
from Falmouth College of Arts in 2001
and Kingston University in 2004.

Sarah loves colour, line, characters, humour,
detail, nature, irony and many cups of tea.
She also paints and writes.

Sarah lives in London and works
from a studio in Forest Hill.

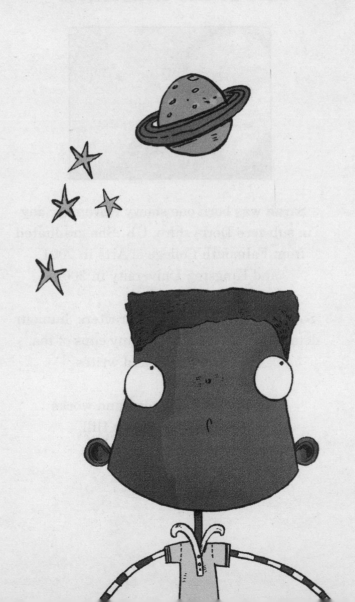